ZOMBIE ZERO
THE SHORT STORIES

MONSTROUS CONSEQUENCES

Zombie Zero: The Short Stories
Monstrous Consequences

ZOMBIE ZERO
THE SHORT STORIES

MONSTROUS CONSEQUENCES

J.K. NORRY

FOREWORD

By the time you read this, we will be pretty deep into the 'Year of the Zombie' for me. We might even be beyond it, as some other book I write pulls you backward through my library; either way, welcome to my idea of what zombies are all about! If you are reading this first, that's fine with me if it's okay with you. There aren't a bunch of spoilers in this book that would ruin any of the others, and there's no need to read them in any order but whatever order you feel compelled to read them in. That being said...

If you like these stories, you are likely to also love 'Zombie Zero: The First Zombie'. That's the first book I wrote in support of this project, and it provides a foundation for the short stories that would have been too much to get into every story. Without that book, these stories are able to stand strong on their own, and in sets; but with that foundation, a lot of holes will get filled in for you. I won't ask you to put this book aside to read it first, but I do hope that this one leads you to that one. And then, to all the others.

You might be the type of person I am, and want to do this in the order it was meant to be done. That would be easy enough: start with 'Zombie Zero: The First Zombie', read the short story volumes in numerical order, and then read 'Zombie Zero: The Last Zombie'. That's how I wrote them, and initially thought of releasing them; but it was better to release the second big book in the midst of the short story releases for a variety of reasons. So don't feel obligated to wait to read 'The Last Zombie' if you are snatching these up as they are released, if you haven't already; feel me being super grateful that you have accompanied me on this crazy year-long zombie escapade...because I am!

The 'Secret Society of Deeper Meaning' came into being this year, and everyone that has joined for free has gotten access to these stories first. With the plan I've got for next year, I'm excited to invite you to join as well.

Unless you're already a member; then you deserve a special thank you, since you didn't have to buy this book to get these stories. I hope to see you stick around, and ring in the new year with me; I've got something very special planned for you.

Also, before we go too into it, I have a story of my own I would like to tell you.

ABOUT THE SHORT STORIES

Let's start out with what folks reading these in order already know, to get it out of the way. This campfire storyteller has a story he wants to tell you. First, there are no spoilers in any of the sections between the stories. Second, you don't have to read them if you don't want to. I liked the idea of sharing a little of the story between the stories with folks who enjoy them, like a lot of my favorite authors often do. If you just want the stories, get to them! There are three of them, and I hope you love them!

For the rest of you, my extended intellectual family, there's something I'd like to share from my past. My joy of reading horror and science fiction pulp publications when I was a kid keeps coming up, as it should with this series, and there's one incident that stands out in my memory.

At about twelve, I announced to my parents that I was an atheist. I should've said that I needed to consider a lot of stuff before I ran around calling myself an 'anything-ist', but I had found a snappy new word.

It got a reaction. Before I knew it, my lazy summer became a youth bible camp; and I was sentenced to two weeks of conversion attempts. It was fine; I had a new pulp book with a bunch of sci-fi and horror stories in it, and a stunning cover that had nothing to do with any of those stories. I stuck it in my backpack, and headed off to camp.

During the first congregational meal, I thought about the story I was reading more than the food I was eating. I couldn't wait to get back and finish it, then get started on the next one. Unbeknownst to me, the counselor in charge of our barracks had left the meal early. He went through our bags, or at least mine, and found something that he needed to talk to me about. He was holding it up when I walked in, pinching it with two fingers like he didn't want to get any on him.

The cover had a clearly undead woman bursting from a lake or similarly peaceful body of water. I'm pretty sure she was missing an eye, and part of her face. At least that's how I remember it. In any case, it was clearly a horror publication. The counselor looked at me like I should be embarrassed that he had found it. He asked if it was mine; I told him that technically it was my Dad's.

He was sure he had me then.

He asked if my Dad knew I had taken it. I told him that since my Dad had literally handed it to me, he probably was fully aware that I had taken it. The counselor was pretty sure I was lying, but he couldn't prove it without my Dad there. He told me that it was not appropriate for me to be reading stories like that, and that he would talk to my Dad when it was time for me to be picked up. We'd get this all straightened out then, he said, two weeks nigh.

In the meantime, he thought it best that he keep the book. I was devastated. For the next two weeks, the only book I could get my hands on was one that no twelve-year-old should be expected to have any interest in at all. Not to knock it; I read most of the Bible as a young man, and it's one of my favorite books to this day. It just didn't interest me at the time. I wanted to find out how much weight the jockey was going to be able to lose during his next big race, and if he would keep having trouble putting it back on.

Is it frustrating not knowing what I'm talking about? It was way more frustrating being partway into a story and having to wait two weeks to find out how it ended. If this was the way God operated, I was pretty sure I wanted my money back.

I sure as Hell wanted my book back. Asking for my money back is the subject of my first book; finally getting my pulp publication back is what this story is about.

I did, too...finally. After two weeks of folks asking why I hadn't accepted someone I had never met as my lord and savior, and badgering me with threats of eternal damnation if I didn't, it was finally over. My folks came to pick me up, and I went right up to my Dad. I pointed at the counselor, who was saying his goodbyes to the other kids.

"He took my book," I said. "He won't give it back to me unless you say it's okay."

My Dad walked right up to the guy.

"Did you take his book?" he asked, all calm.

The guy nodded, started to explain himself. My Dad cut him off.

"Give it back," he said, still calm.

The guy looked at me.

"Are you sure you still want it, after the last two weeks?" he asked.

"Give it back," my Dad said again, slightly less calm.

The lion turned to a lamb before me, went back to the bunkhouse and got my book. Things turned out fine, after all.

Unfortunately, the jockey didn't make it.

ODE TO SEAN HARRINGTON

The artist that we chose to do the cover for 'Zombie Zero: The First Zombie' and 'Zombie Zero: The Last Zombie' was an awesome pick for those covers. As soon as I saw his art, I loved his style. We were delighted at how quickly he got back to us, and how professionally he fielded our request for the first cover. I sent him a long email and a sketch that looked like one of our dogs had drawn it, and we waited.

Oh, it was so cool! So was the next one, the cover for 'The Last Zombie'. I gave him strong suggestions, again; he over-delivered, again. We couldn't wait to see what the covers for these were going to be, since I had sent him story synopses instead of cover art ideas this time; but there was really nothing else for us to do. So wait we did, until the art started coming in at regular intervals. Every timeframe that he estimated throughout this whole year was dead on, or he delivered early. Watching such a talented artist represent his work with such professionalism was almost as rewarding as receiving the art itself.

This cover jumped out at us in a special way. The people that he creates come off just as textured and multifaceted as the characters in these stories, and this was such a fantastic depiction of exactly that depth. The image forever frozen in time by Sean Harrington for this book cover is dynamic and suspenseful and wonderful. Even knowing how the situation turns out doesn't stop me from being a little shocked when I look at it, in the most delightful way.

Some might think it's a weird dream, to want to publish a series of books that harken back to the pulp publications I loved so much as a kid. I won't argue the strangeness or lack thereof in any of my desires; I've never had a drive to be a normal. I devoured science fiction and horror publications when I was a kid, marveling at the art on the covers and the stories inside. Those publications found a place in my heart, and live there to this day. Very few aspects of those publications bothered me, and we changed those things.

The print editions of these are printed on fine quality paper. Also, the art actually always has something to do with the stories. Sean Harrington helped me make this dream come true, and I am very grateful to him for that. Thanks again, Sean!

ODE TO DAWN MARSHALL

You may know me from my books, which is a great way to get to know me. If you know me through my blog, or Sudden Insight Publishing, or over scotch, you already know I have a partner. The thing I think is important to note is that my partner is more than the love of my life, or my favorite person in the world...she's those things, too; but those are not the only high-ranking positions she holds in my life.

Her name is Dawn Marshall, and she plays a very vital role in making all my dreams come true. Actually, she plays several very vital roles; but I am all about popping up gigantic umbrellas for lots of things to fall under. When we first met, I was not a big fan of spotting what was good for me. Later, I looked back and realized what a good thing I had briefly had with her. I coaxed her back into my life, and dedicated myself to winning her heart, and I'm glad for it every day.

As my muse, Dawn somehow never hears too many irrelevant details pertaining to the strange stuff I keep stored in my head.

As my editor, she knows exactly when I need to pull back or push forward; she's completely honest about which of my books are her favorites as a reader, and she always echoes the voice in my head telling me to put something in or take something out. That's proofreader and beta reader extraordinaire, if we're counting. She was the one who decided we needed to start a company, and who took on the task of learning all the technical aspects of publishing so we might publish both my books and others'.

Dawn's big heart caused mine to grow somewhere along the way, and make room for her giant furry buddy. His name is Mammoth, and he and I went from uneasy comrades to best of friends while Dawn brokered the connection. After a while, I started to think he might like a little sister.

That big heart of Dawn's came to the rescue, and she suggested we check out the local SPCA. We found Ximena there, an adorable little mystery mix that will forever look like a mini black lab. We took her home, and a strongly bonded family formed while we were busy making sure we all loved our lives together. There is a loving conspiracy going on in my home. I couldn't be more grateful to its mastermind, or her big heart.

ABOUT IAN'S SHAME

When this set come along in my writing queue, there were two already completed. They would turn out to be the last and first to be published, respectively. The sequence was decided in part by the timeline and in part by the nature of the tie-ins.

'The Sickness Spreads' clearly needed to come first, followed by 'The Beginning of the End'. The third volume to fall in place was 'Love Lost at Sea', and those first three volumes answered some questions raised in 'Zombie Zero: The First Zombie'.

'The Zombie Killers' came next, to give us a bigger peek into the lives of some very brave men and women fighting this outbreak. That tie-in was strong, but not necessarily a question every reader might have asked while reading 'The First Zombie'. This set started with a question that I asked myself while the first book was still in progress, and is largely responsible for seeding this whole idea in the first place. The question kept nagging at me, until I looked through a special portal in my mind and answered it.

As soon as I had, I knew I needed to share.

This set bled into the one I wrote before and the one I wrote after, in a couple ways. Actually, the second story in this set was the first one I got started on, to answer that question that the main story had brought up for me. It got finished before this one, but that was not the right order to share them in. The other story in this set got finished first, but that struck me as a great finale to the set. Then the next story in the next set called to me, and I got to work on writing 'Kirsten's Dream' from 'Love Lost at Sea'. It showed me what I had been running from, and sent me back to finish this story with a fresh perspective.

We'll talk about that, after you read the story. Right now I would ask that you judge this fellow on his thoughts more than his actions, and consider that his situation is way more common than you or I might like to think. Not the zombie apocalypse part of it, of course...I mean the thing that fills Ian's thoughts with both intense joy and extreme darkness, and has taken his life to a place he never thought possible.

I'm referring to 'Ian's Shame', of course.

I hope you love it!

(The story, not the shame.)

IAN'S SHAME

Biting his lip, curling his body around the pain, Ian fought the dull twisting ache in his belly. He felt the slow trembling weakness of his muscles as he tried to reach out, to pull his jacket tighter about his body. Shivering, he ducked deeper into the darkness as he heard footsteps and voices approaching the alley.

"Oy, Davey," he heard a man say. "Looks like we might be set for awhile."

There was the rumpling sound of cellophane, someone rifling through a plastic bag; then came the sounds of a scuffle, feet moving quickly followed by the low dull thud of a fist striking, or someone being thrown against a wall.

"Dammit, man," another voice said. "Don't be announcing our good fortune to the whole bleeding country."

"Leave off, then," the first voice spoke again, in a strangled tone. There was another series of scuffling sounds, the plastic crumpling again.

"I'll keep those," the second voice said gruffly.

"Of course, of course," the first man said, his voice lower. "Can we take a couple now? Y'know, take the edge off?"

Ian leaned forward without thinking. The twisting need within him was too much for him to sit still, and that familiar phrase drew him out of the shadows.

"Hush!" the man named Davey said. "I heard something."

His voice dropped to a low whisper, but Ian could still hear.

"Behind that trash bin," Davey murmured. "You see something?"

"Could be one of them," the other man replied.

"It's one of the slow ones, if it is," Davey replied. "If it was one of the fast ones, we would be dinner by now."

Ian heard footsteps, coming closer.

"Oy!" one of them shouted. "Who's back there?"

Unwinding himself, Ian slowly dragged his aching bones to a sagging standing position. He teetered in place, dragged one foot forward, and toppled forward. Barely catching himself, he felt the sudden pained shock of the impact followed by the aching agony of a good tooth rattling. Slowly, painfully, he dragged himself to his feet once more.

"It's one of them," the one that wasn't Davey said.

Davey shook his head.

"You're wrong," he said. "Take a closer look. He's not a zombie. Our friend here is dopesick. Aren't you, buddy?"

Ian gazed at him through the thick fog of cotton that used to be his brain. He hated that word; the first time he had heard it, Ian had laughed at the man saying it. Ian had told him that dopamine withdrawal was virtually identical to the flu, and that only a weak doper would succumb to using it as an excuse not to get out of bed. The first time he had experienced it, months later, Ian had lost every bit of upright morality he had thought he'd had. When his mind had finally come back to him, he had been in an alley with a needle sticking from his arm.

"Yeah," Ian muttered. His voice was thick and hoarse and nearly unintelligible. "I'm dopesick. So what?"

"So we got some pills," Davey dug a bottle from his pocket, shook it. "It's the good stuff, too. No acetaminophen."

Ian lurched toward them. "Where did you get that?"

"Oh, no," Davey said, backing away. "First I need to know what you're willing to do for a couple of these babies."

"Anything," Ian sputtered, without hesitating. "You know what I'll do for them. I'll do anything."

Davey chuckled. "That's right," he said. "You'll get on your knees and bark like a dog, that's what you'll do."

Ian frowned. He glanced down at his slacks, then at the dirty street.

"I'd really rather not," he murmured.

Davey's companion squealed with laughter.

"I'd really rather not," he sang, losing his Irish brogue to mock Ian's English accent.

Davey elbowed him, hard.

"Shut up, you fool," he said. "You want to get eaten?"

The man looked around, startled.

"They haven't shown up anywhere in Europe," he said, quietly. His voice was trembling, and he sounded uncertain.

Ian didn't know what he was talking about, and he didn't care. He wanted those pills. Dropping to his knees, he looked up at Davey.

"Is this what you want?" he asked, quietly.

Davey bent over, sneered at him. Ian could smell his breath; it was rank and rotten, stinking of stale beer and bitter coffee, mixed with milk and gone sour. He resisted the urge to gag.

"Not so fancy now, Englishman," he breathed. "Are ya?"

"No." Ian held his breath. "Not so fancy at all."

"Bark like a dog, Englishman," Davey sneered, wafting a fresh cloud of sour stink his way. Ian thought of pointing out that he had just shushed his companion for being too loud twice; he imagined the conversation that might ensue, and sighed.

Ian frowned. "Bark," he said, quietly.

"Come now, Englishman, you can do better than that." Davey opened the bottle of pills. He popped one in his mouth.

Ian barked like a dog, like a little dog begging for a treat.

Davey chuckled. "Good boy. Open your mouth."

Ian opened his mouth. He tried not to think of where those fingers might have been, or how rarely they had likely been washed. When he felt the pill on his tongue at last, he closed his mouth and swallowed. Ian closed his eyes for a moment as it went down. He knew that the effects would be delayed, and that there was no actual reason for him to feel the euphoria already creeping in. There it was, though, a magical feeling in his throat that defied such claims; folks had told him that it was psychological, feeling instant relief from a pill that would take several minutes to become active in his bloodstream. Ian didn't care; euphoria was euphoria, and he'd take it any way he could get it.

"You want another?"

Ian's eyes flashed open. He nodded, helplessly.

Davey laughed. "Big bark this time, boy. Big bark!"

Ian lunged forward, woofed at him.

Davey struck him, a hard backhand that nearly sent him sprawling.

"Bad dog!" Davey sneered. "Big friendly bark, bad dog!"

Trembling, Ian looked up at him. He woofed, quietly.

"Good boy." Davey nodded. He placed another pill on Ian's tongue, and Ian gulped it down.

"Stand up, Englishman." Davey was smiling an open and friendly grin at him, extending his hand to help.

Ian took his hand, stood shakily.

"Davey," the other man said. "Hey,

Davey. Can I have one too?"

Davey's eyes went cold. He turned, glared at the man.

"You got no manners," Davey admonished him. "You need to learn a lesson from our new friend here. Tilt your head back."

He did as he was told, immediately. Davey placed a single pill carefully on the tip of his bulbous nose.

"Now you be a good boy, and leave that there while we talk," Davey said, his voice edged with anger. "If it falls, you will regret it. Pay attention, boy, and watch how polite folk interact."

Davey turned to Ian. A change came over him. He smiled, stuck out his hand and winked at Ian.

"Hello, old boy," Davey said. "My name's Davey. My socially inept companion is called Rory. What's your name, then?"

Ian blinked. He glanced at Rory; he was still balancing the pill on the end of his nose. He grasped Davey's outstretched hand.

"Nice to meet you, Davey," he said. "I'm Ian."

"Oy, now there's a handshake!" Davey pumped Ian's hand. "You want another pill, Ian?"

Ian glanced at Rory again. He nodded.

"Oh, don't worry about him," Davey chuckled. "Just a little fun between friends."

He dropped another pill into Ian's palm; Ian popped it in his mouth.

Davey nodded, glanced at Rory.

"Good boy," he chuckled. "Eat up."

Rory moved his head forward just enough for the pill to fall into his mouth. He held it on his tongue for a moment, then closed his mouth over the treat. It was obviously not the first time he had done the trick.

"Come on, boys," Davey waved them on down the street. "We got work to do."

Ian stood his ground, watching after them. Davey stopped after a few steps, glanced at Rory and then spoke to Ian.

"Come on, Ian," Davey growled.

"Where are we going?" Ian asked

"To get more pills," Davey snapped. "Obviously."

"Where?" Ian was feeling much better; that didn't mean he felt one hundred percent mentally. That was a number he had left behind long ago. He had gone from being annoyed with the responsibility of often being the brightest person in the room to feeling like the conversation had left him behind enough to get used to it. Sometimes he could barely form words these days, or understand them. It only happened when he'd had way too little, or way too much; but it still happened.

Davey looked at him in bewilderment for a full minute; finally he shook his head, spoke quietly.

"Do you know what's going on, old boy?" Davey asked, not unkindly.

Ian felt a cold prickle claw its way down his spine. He shook his head.

Davey laughed. He looked over at Rory; Rory shook his head, laughed uneasily.

"The cops is on strike," Rory said. He looked slyly at Davey.

"Aye," Davey nodded, watching Ian. "That they are."

Ian's eyes went round. "Are you sure?"

Davey reached behind him, pulled a revolver from his pants and held it in the air. He fired off a round.

Ian flinched, his face going white. His ears were ringing, and his buzz was being tainted in the worst way by this whole experience. He took a step back, putting more distance between them.

"Where did you get that?" Ian stared at the weapon, terrified.

"What, this?" Davey waved it around, causing Ian to back up yet another step. "I've had it awhile. Don't worry, Ian. I won't shoot you. I don't shoot my friends. You're my friend; aren't you, Ian?"

Ian nodded, dumbly.

"Why are the police on strike?" he asked.

Davey crossed the space between them in three easy strides, clapped him on the back. He grinned.

"It's the end of the world, don't you know," Davey elbowed him.

"Yeah, sure," Ian said. "Everyone knows that. Nearly everyone is starving, or at war, or strung out on something."

Ian hung his head dejectedly; he didn't see the bemused look that the other two men exchanged.

"Right," Davey chuckled. He clapped Ian on the back again. "So let's go get us some more pills."

Ian raised his eyes enough to look at Davey.

"Won't there be other looters?" he asked.

"Aye," Davey nodded. He waved the pistol in the air. "They probably won't have one of these."

Ian knitted his eyebrows together.

"You'll be the lookout," Davey said. "You see trouble coming, you take care of it or holler at us and run. No danger. No breaking the laws that no longer apply."

Ian sighed. "Can I have a couple more of those pills?"

* * *

"Loyalty." Davey walked a half a step ahead of them. Ian floated along with Rory, trailing in his wake on either side. It felt like floating because Ian had finally gotten enough pills in his belly that everything felt like some version of floating. Finally. His thoughts floated about in his head; they were disconnected and vague, but weighted with a meaning he couldn't discern. His arms floated at his sides, his feet floated over the sidewalk. Davey's voice floated to his ears.

"It's the most important thing, don't you think?" Davey asked.

Ian glanced over at the gun in the back of Davey's pants. He thought about the pills in Davey's pocket. He nodded, his head floating.

"Loyalty," Ian repeated. "Absolutely. Most important thing."

Davey threw him a doubtful look, one eyebrow arched.

"You're a clever one; aren't you,

Englishman?" he asked.

Ian shrugged. "I like to think so. Doesn't everyone?"

"Not Rory," Davey snapped. "Hey Rory, you clever?"

"Not me," Rory chuckled. "I'm dumb as a box o rocks."

"Well," Ian conceded. "I never said I wasn't dumb. I simply admitted to being clever. There may have been a time when I felt that my cleverness outweighed my own stupidity, but that time has long since passed. There was a time when I thought that one could not exist without the other, which put both in context and made my occasional lack of cleverness acceptable. Now I see that one can exist without the other. I am forced to admit, in all honesty, that is has been some time indeed since I did anything I might categorize as clever."

Rory exchanged a look with Davey.

"Oy," Rory sputtered, shaking his head. "That was some clever talk right there. Don't you think, Davey?"

"Oy," Davey echoed his agreement. He glared at Ian for a moment as they continued walking together.

"Really," Ian sputtered. "I'm really quite dumb."

He eyed the pistol sticking from Davey's pants again. He listened to the hypnotizing rattle of pills shaking about in their bottle, in Davey's pocket. Ian wondered why he was the only one who could see that his mere presence in the conversation implied his inability to make good decisions. A truly clever man would never find himself in this position; he knew that. How could they not?

"I used to be an engineer," Ian said quietly. "Then I got hurt, and I had to have knee surgery. After it healed I couldn't stop taking the pills. My prescription ran out, so I started buying them on the black market. Then my dealer ran out of pills one day, and offered me some heroin instead. There was no going back from there. I stopped showing up for work, or I'd nod at my desk for hours. They sacked me. I lost my house, my family disowned me. Then I ran out of the few dollars I had stolen or borrowed, ran out of pills and powder, and ended up on the street."

"Are we having a meeting?" Rory piped up. "Aren't ye supposed to start with 'Hello, they call me Ian; I'm a slave to the float'?"

Ian wasn't floating anymore. The whole conversation was bringing him down. He honestly never thought he would find himself making a case for his own lack of intelligence.

"No," Ian frowned. "I'm not confessing. I'm simply telling it like it is. A clever man would have lived his life differently. This is where I belong."

Rory cackled; Davey stayed oddly silent. He glanced at each of them from time to time, but he didn't say anything.

"Sounds like you think you're better than us," Rory sniffed.

"On the contrary," Ian replied. "I was dopesick and on the street when you two found me. You, on the other hand, both have a friend and a purpose. And pills. I cannot claim such riches. I look up to the man who does, I appreciate the hand of friendship when he extends it; but I have nothing to offer in trade, no wealth that I might compare to yours. I have only hope, for the mercy of those much greater than me."

For a long quiet moment they walked. Rory looked confused, Davey appeared deep in thought, and Ian let his concern hang on his face. Without breaking stride, Davey pulled the bottle of pills from his pocket and gave Rory one. Then he glanced at Ian, nodded, and gave him one. Davey took one for himself. He stopped, pointed.

"See that window?" he asked.

It was the first storefront they had passed that didn't have its glass shattered and its front door pried open, other than the few locked behind bars or grated metal until further notice. There were no lights on inside, and the magical prescription symbol was displayed prominently on the window. A network of thin wires was laid out between two thick sheets of glass; looking closer Ian saw that it was not undamaged. Two cobwebs of shatter marred the smooth surface; one reached a long cracked tendril across the length of the window. The door was glass, but covered over by a second door made of wrought iron; they weren't getting through there without a key.

"How do we get inside?" Ian breathed. They all three stared at the darkened window, their eyes wide as the wheels turned; they looked like sinners glimpsing heaven for the first time, plotting a way to break in.

"Davey," Rory whispered, his voice touched with awe. "You gonna shoot the lock off the door?"

Ian opened his mouth, to let flow a sarcastic retort. Instead he shut it, looked at Davey. He was learning.

"You can," Davey said. He pulled out the

pistol, reversed it and held the handle out to Rory. "When the ricochet kills you, or the lock gets permanently fixed in place, or you draw attention to the job we got here, I'll take the gun back and split the rest of the pills with someone who doesn't think we're on a bloody Hollywood movie set. Ian? Any ideas?"

Davey put the pistol back in his pants, rather than offer it to him as well. Ian shrugged, nodded to the window.

"I think the window is our best point of entry, as you stated earlier," Ian said. Davey nodded, and he went on. "We can't shatter it, though; we need to remove the entire thing. That means we need something bigger than a stone, or a bullet."

Davey nodded. He stepped to a nearby automobile, pulled out the pistol again, and shattered the driver's side window. He reached his arm through the opening, unlocked the door and opened it. Ignoring the shards of glass, he sat in the seat and began punching buttons. On the third button, the boot creaked open. Davey got out, threw the lid of the trunk the rest of the way open, and dug around in its depths. First he pulled a spare from the shadows; he rolled it at Rory, too fast and wobbly for him to catch it. Rory angled his body to stop it from rolling past him; it struck his knee, and he cried out. Davey sniggered as it wobbled to a still stop at Rory's feet. Next was a tire iron; he tossed it at Ian.

Ian threw up his hands; the metal rod hit one of his hands, then the opposite forearm. He bit his lip to keep from crying out, bent to retrieve it where it had fallen. Davey was chuckling as he straightened.

"Catch!" Davey sneered. He pointed to the window. "Get to work!"

Grasping the tire with both hands, Rory lifted it to his shoulder and ran at the window. He stopped just short, planted his feet and flung the tire at the glass.

"Rory, don't-" Ian spoke, too late.

The tire left his hands, flew at the window and bounced off unceremoniously. It caught Rory at the knees, spilling him backward into the street. Ian went to him, bent over him.

"Are you all right?" Ian asked, extending his hand.

"I'm fine." Rory batted it away. He got to his feet, shakily. "Your turn."

Ian looked down at the metal bar in his other hand. He shrugged, walked to the window and began worrying at the outer frame with the slim prying end. Working his way along the bottom of the window, Ian separated the wood and metal and stripping holding the grated glass in place. He kept prying it away after reaching the corner, peeling off pieces and tossing them behind him. When he was nearly to the top, Ian felt a tap on his shoulder. He turned.

"Let me have a go," Rory said, holding out his hand. "You're taking too long."

Ian glanced at Davey; he shrugged, nodded. Handing the tire iron over to him, Ian tried to be helpful.

"If you just keep prying at the-" he began.

"Shut up, Englishman," Rory snapped. "I got this."

He stepped to the window and swung the rod at the center. It bounced off, nearly coming out of his hands. Rory struck it again, then a third time in the same place.

"Rory, that's not going to work," Ian said.

Rory hit the glass once more. It crackled, and a tiny network of broken tendrils spread from the small blemish. He grinned, and threw a triumphant look at Ian; then he attacked the window with renewed vigor, striking it several times in a row.

"Enough," Davey called out. "You tried. You failed. Give it back to Ian."

It looked like he wanted to argue, or advance on the glass again. Instead Rory sighed and held the tire iron out to him. Ian worked at the framing until three sides were in pieces at his feet. He wedged the slim metal under the exposed glass, wiggling it until it began to slide forward. Stepping to one side, he worked it away from the frame; moving to the other, it took very little effort to slide it the rest of the way out. Once he got it going, Ian stepped back and let the sheet fall to the street. It shattered, but kept its shape around the grated network.

"Oy!" Rory charged forward, began scrambling over the frame.

Davey eyed Ian, and finally nodded.

"You want to go in?" Davey asked him.

Ian spread his hands. "I thought you needed a lookout."

"Hold up!" Davey's voice stopped Rory halfway between finally getting a leg up and completely tumbling into the shop. Rory perched awkwardly on the sill, gazing back at Davey.

"You trust him?" Davey asked.

Ian shrugged. "I trust you."

Davey nodded, satisfied. He ran at the opening, placed his hands on it as he leapt, and pommelled into the store. A moment later, he was at the window pushing Rory back into the street. Davey laughed as Rory hit the sheet of glass, shattering it further; it held its shape, and he rolled to the sidewalk in a tumbled heap.

"Keep an eye out," Davey said, looking down at Rory. His gaze drifted to Ian. "Come on, Englishman."

Ian wasn't floating quite enough to think he could leap the barrier like Davey had; yet he wasn't about to ooze over it like Rory had been about to. Standing the spare tire upright, he rolled it next to the wall and used it as a step. He saw Rory watching him as he dropped easily into the shop; the man looked less than pleased. Ian flashed him a quick smile.

"Be right back," he said, and followed Davey. They approached a locked door in the back, metal door in a metal frame. Davey rapped heavily on it. He cocked an eyebrow at Ian, spoke quietly.

"Once we open this door an alarm will probably sound."

Ian nodded. "Okay. Do we need to move fast?"

"Nah," Davey waved his hand dismissively. "I just didn't want it to startle ye, that's all."

"How do we get in?" Ian asked.

Davey dug in his pocket, straightened a folding knife in his hands. He nodded toward the door handle before moving in on it.

"There's a quarter inch space there, exposing the latch," he shrugged. "That's why I assume they have an alarm; that, and because these wonderful little rooms usually do."

Slipping the knife easily into the wide crack, Davey popped the lock as easily as if he'd used a key. There were fluorescents overhead, and they came on automatically when they sensed the motion. For several glorious seconds Ian stared at huge containers of pills bathed in bright heavenly light. Then the alarm sounded, and he jumped.

Davey laughed. "You know what we're looking for?"

"Oh, yeah." Ian grinned, and moved to the nearest row of dispensers. "Should we grab some bottles or..."

"Oy," Davey nodded. "Go find some bottles."

Neither of them fooled the other, or thought they were. After a few minutes of searching, they both had unsightly bulges already forming in most of their pockets. Ian had found a couple cloth shopping bags, and filled them with empty bottles. They stood side by side for some time, filling containers like they were professionals placing orders. There was no counting how many bottles they had filled, or how many pills they had popped during the process, when they heard Rory calling out.

"Davey!" His voice was faint, strained with urgency.

"In here!" Davey moved toward the door, grabbed Rory and pulled him inside.

"Somebody's here!" Rory whispered. "They're coming through the front door. They got keys, Davey."

"Yeah?" Davey brandished his pistol. "They got a gun?"

Rory shook his head, and Ian felt his face go a shade paler.

"I don't know," Rory answered. "I didn't see one."

Davey handed Rory the bag he had been filling.

"Well," he said, "let's see if they shoot back."

Ian moved between Davey and the door.

"I'll go first, boss." Ian tried a smile. "Draw their fire."

Davey glanced at him, then at Rory. He nodded.

"Go on, then," Davey said.

Ian went through the doorway, took three bold steps into the unlighted shop. He couldn't see anything; as his eyes adjusted to the lack of florescence, Ian called out into the darkness.

"We have a gun!" he cried. "We don't want to shoot anybody; but we will if you get our way, or try and stop us. I suggest you clear out and go on home to what you've got left there."

His eyes caught movement, a shadow within a shadow. He heard the sound of a door being opened, followed by the sound of that same door swinging shut. Taking a half step back, he felt Davey's gun press against his back.

"I think they're gone," he whispered, stepping forward again.

"Then why are ye whispering?" Rory asked, cackling.

Dave elbowed him. "Because it might be a trap."

The pills were really kicking in now, and Ian was beginning to feel a little more invincible than the recommended dosage would have caused. He strode confidently to the door, swung it open, and walked outside. No one tried to stop him, and there was nobody waiting to jump him on the street. There was someone watching, across the street and swathed in shadows: Ian peered that direction, trying to make out details.

As Davey stepped up beside him, Rory bumped into Ian. He bounced off, giggling, while Davey gazed across the street.

"What do ye see?" Davey hissed, elbowing Rory.

"Somebody," Ian shrugged. "I don't know. I can't tell."

The shadowed form drifted away.

"Looked like a lady to me," Rory said.

"Oy?" Davey asked, and Rory nodded. "Come on, then. This one's got the eyes of a hawk. If he says it's a lady, it's a lady."

Rory nodded again, more excitedly.

"Aye," he said. "A pretty lady too."

Davey sneered, gave him another painful elbow. He nudged Ian too.

"That I don't believe," Davey said. "I seen some of the ladies he said was pretty. Come on."

He started walking, and Rory fell in step beside him. Ian was left standing alone in the street again, biting his lip and surfing his high. Davey stopped, whirled on him and drew the pistol.

"You coming?"

"Yeah," Ian stammered. "Yeah, yeah, of course."

He ran a few steps, slowed to a walking pace as he got in front of them. Ian waved them forward, pointing to movement in the street.

"She went that way," he whispered.

Davey pushed past him, grabbing the bag that Ian had shouldered roughly as he passed. Ian let it go, watched him pass it to Rory.

"Look after that," Davey said.

Ian trailed behind a half of a step, sullenly digging in his pocket while he walked. He dug out three pills, swallowed them dry. He was beginning to feel like his old self again. Not his old, old self: not the respectable and proper and promising young man he had been a year ago; but his old self, able to conduct himself with some sort of normalcy without feeling like he was dying, or wishing he would.

"There she goes," Rory hissed.

Ian felt Davey grab his sleeve, and pull him roughly along. He got more annoyed with every step, watching his sweater stretch and feeling his last nerve fray. Pushing Davey away just as they stopped in a darkened alley, Ian tugged his sleeve back into shape as he dug in his pocket for another pill.

"It's a dead end, little lady," Davey called out, stepping further from Ian and deeper into the alley. Ian looked behind him, desperately, then caught eyes with Rory.

Rory narrowed his eyes, shook his head.

"Come on, now," Davey said. "Come on out."

"Leave me alone!"

The voice was trembling, brave and frightened at the same time. Davey stepped forward, opening his mouth again, and she burst from the shadows. Running straight at Davey, she leaned forward and shouldered him aside as she passed. He bumped off Rory just as she breezed by Ian; he stepped back, in surprise at the sudden movement.

"Go!" Davey cried at him, pulling out his pistol and waving it, as he tripped over Rory where he had fallen. "Get her!"

Ian ran. He went in the direction that she had gone, fully intending to peel off and get the hell away from Davey as soon as he was out of sight. The panicked sound of footsteps on wooden planking drew his attention, and he followed her further than he had planned. He saw her slip into someone's backyard, then into a storage shed.

Stopping on the long bridge, Ian stood

and waited for Davey and Rory to catch up. They were gasping for air from the short run, and their feet fell hard and slow as they approached him.

"Tell me," Davey snarled, "that ye didn't lose her."

Ian shook his head, pointed downward.

"Afraid so, boss," he said loudly. He winked at Davey, and nudged Rory with his elbow, in case they were more daft even than he had supposed. Pointing exaggeratedly downward again, he went on.

"I suppose we'd best give up," he called out, pointing.

Rory went to the side, leaned over. Davey gave Ian a sideways glance, then followed.

Ian dashed forward, seized the butt of the pistol in Davey's waistband, and pulled it free. He backed up while Davey whirled, and advanced on him; then he tossed it over the railing, and ran. The sounds of footsteps were right behind him; Ian was tackled just after he heard the satisfying splash far below. Davey was on top of him then, his face red and right up in Ian's. He grasped Ian's collar with both hands and shook him. Ian's head made a dull thumping every time it hit the bridge. It took a few painful thuds for him to realize that Davey was speaking, and that a word accompanied each strike.

"You. Find. Her." Davey's voice was an angry growl. "Or. I. Kill. You. Get. It? You. Find. He-"

Ian nodded, tried to throw him off.

"I got it," he cried, wrapping his arms protectively about his head. He stayed there, curled into himself, until Davey had stood and given him a good kick in the ribs.

"Alright," he heard Davey say. "Get up."

Ian struggled to his feet, tried to clear the ringing from his ears. Before he could get his balance Davey shoved him, and he staggered a few feet along the bridge. He shook his head.

"Not that way," Ian said, rubbing at the back of his skull. He walked past Davey, giving him a wide berth, and approached the far end of the crossing. He pointed at the backyard, then put his finger to his lips.

"Quiet?" Davey laughed. "You tossed my gun; you didn't change the odds. Where did she go?"

"I don't know for sure," Ian lied. "I saw her go into this yard, and I didn't see her come back out."

Bright light stabbed at his eyes suddenly.

"I got us a couple torches at the drugstore," Rory boasted.

Davey snatched one, and soon two beams were spearing Ian's face.

"That's not helping," he pointed out. "Let's have us a look around."

"Rory, check the hedges," Davey said, "and watch the street, make sure she doesn't run off again. Ian, come with me."

Davey directly moved to the shed, glancing back to make sure Ian was with him. He cried out as the door squeaked open.

"Oy!" Davey said. "Let's have us a look in here."

Spearing the ray of light into the shadows, Davey turned to Ian. He was frowning.

"See anything?" Ian asked. He had seen the tarp, had seen it moving; had Davey seen it too? Was he waiting for Ian to point out the obvious?

Davey shone the light over the small space again, pausing momentarily on the tarp as he moved the torch in his hand.

"Nothing in here," Davey said. He turned.

Ian sighed. "Did you look under that tarp?"

"Nah," Davey waved his hand dismissively. "Think she's under there?"

Ian shrugged. "It's probably worth checking."

Davey nodded, leaned forward.

"Are you hiding in there, pretty lady?" he called out.

Davey took a step toward the covering, his light trained on it.

"That tarp just moved," Ian pointed out. "She's under there."

Davey kept protesting, and Ian kept insisting, until he pulled the tarp off her huddled form. Ian's ears were still ringing, and he tuned out their heated exchange while he tried to shake it off. Davey antagonized her for a full minute, until she leapt to her feet and attacked him. Ian caught her as she tried to escape the shed, held her as Davey recovered his feet. She lost her balance, and struggled mightily against his grip. As she got her feet under her, she struggled with renewed strength. Rory came up behind, and the words he and Davey exchanged were lost on Ian's foggy brain as he held her. He heard Rory suggest that he drag her out into the open, and a few moments later he pushed her down into the lawn.

They lined up shoulder to shoulder, Rory and Davey both training their flashlights on her. Davey leaned forward, and spoke.

"Hey girlie," he sneered. "You know what I-"

Davey crumpled to the ground, silent. Ian

moved forward, as Rory began screaming. He didn't check for a pulse, or try to turn him over; instead, he grasped the strap of the cloth bag slung over Davey's shoulder. Looking up from his tugging, he realized that she was pointing a gun at him. He let go the bag, backed up a step.

Ian's head spun with concussed confusion. He stared at Davey, realizing that he was dead somehow; his eyes went to her, realizing she had gotten a gun somehow. None of it added up. He frowned fiercely, collected his thoughts as best as he could.

"Alright, now, hold on," Ian said, spreading his hands before him. He glanced at the bag, moved toward it slowly. "Just because the cops are striking doesn't mean we can't be civilized toward each other. Just let me-"

"Back off," she said. She held the gun on him, steady.

Ian took a step back; Rory laughed.

"Careful," he said, stepping forward. "You might accidentally-"

The young woman shifted slightly. There was a click and then a boom, and the grass at Rory's feet exploded. He leapt backward.

"If I shoot you, it will not be an accident," she assured him.

A hungry howl split the air, a wolf or coyote calling out from far off. The woman turned her head for a moment, to look to the sky. Ian scrambled to his feet and ran; after a few minutes he heard the sound of Rory panting behind him. He ran faster, pushing his heaving lungs and his burning legs, until he heard Rory stop behind him. Gasping for air, he called out after Ian.

"Oy!" Rory heaved in a lungful of air. "Oy! Ian! Stop!"

He shook the bag of pills that he was still carrying, and Ian felt his feet slow to a walk. He stopped, sighed and turned, and began walking back to Rory. Digging in his pockets, trying to count what wasn't smashed or in his belly, Ian quickened his pace.

"Let me have some now," Ian said, as forcefully as he could.

Rory chuckled, still panting.

"Maybe you want to do a trick for me," he sneered.

Turning on his heel, Ian strode purposefully from Rory's heaving breaths.

"Come on back, then," Rory called out, more clearly. "I'm just giving ye a hard time."

Ian stopped, but he didn't turn.

"No tricks?" he called over his shoulder. "No silly games?"

"No silly games," Rory echoed. "Now that Davey is gone, we can be friends. Here, take it."

Ian turned around, stepped forward and took the bag. He slung it over his elbow and pulled out a bottle. Shaking out a half dozen pills onto his palm, he held it out to Rory.

Rory smiled, and took two. "I'd like to take more, but I want to go somewhere. I was hoping you'd come; I think you'll like it"

Ian took the other four pills, capped the bottle and dropped it back in the bag. He returned it to Rory.

"Where?" he asked.

"A store I used to work at," Rory shrugged. "I know a way in. There should be food and water there. We can lock ourselves in, stay safe and get annihilated."

"Okay," Ian nodded. "Sounds good. Do you really think the strike has made it that dangerous?"

Rory narrowed his eyes, as if trying to figure out if Ian was putting him on about something. Then he shook his head, smiled.

"No offense, lad," he sighed, "but for a smart guy you're pretty dumb. It's extremely dangerous to be in a position that cannot be defended during a situation of this nature."

Ian nodded. "All right, then. You don't

have to go all military on me. What were you, army?"

"Aye." Rory nodded, chuckled under his breath. "A lifetime ago."

He started walking, and Ian fell into step beside him.

*   *   *

Ian had been high before. He had taken an excess of pain pills more times than he could count, had jammed a needle in his arm to experience the most sublime euphoria of his lifetime, and had spent more than one interminable stretches of minutes wondering whether his heart was about to stop. He'd been high before, plenty of times. This was a whole new level.

The place was perfect, a ground floor store with an apartment above it. No one was there, for some reason, and Ian was too caught up in delighting at the layout to wonder why. They barricaded all the doors, kept away from the windows all night, and took pills like they were breaths. During the day they gazed out at the empty street below, popping pills and swapping stories. Rory had been right; with Davey gone, the dynamic was different. Floating together on a continual cloud, Rory and Ian became fast friends. They were looking out the window, lost in time and high as they could be, when they saw her below.

Rory stiffened in his seat, leaned forward to watch her walk by.

"Well, hell," he said. "That's that girl."

Ian nodded. "Looks like she found herself a protector. See the size of that dog?"

Rory stood up, moved to the door and began unstacking furniture.

"What are you doing?" Ian asked.

"Following her."

"Why?" Ian frowned. "She has a gun, and a dog."

"Exactly." Rory tossed aside more items as he spoke. "She don't need both. We need to get that gun."

"Why?" Ian repeated.

Rory stopped as he cleared away the last piece, a dresser that squealed as its legs slid across the floor.

"Ian," he said, looking at the floor. "I haven't been completely honest with you. I don't have time to bring you up to speed on the state of the world, but it's bad. Really bad. We need that gun if we want to have any chance at surviving. I'm going; you come with me if you want."

He opened the door, stepped through it and looked back. Ian frowned, and followed.

Ian called out to him as they descended to the ground floor.

"You're not going to hurt her, are you?" he asked.

Rory chuckled. Ian didn't like the dark rolling sound.

"No more than I got to," Rory responded.

"You're not going to-"

"Hush!" Rory snapped. "Don't be walking into the street gabbing and carrying on. Shut up or stay behind."

Ian followed him into the street. He took a couple more pills, to make sure all this walking around didn't stomp out the clouds under his feet. Each time Rory turned to him, or motioned him to move or hurry up, Ian smiled or followed the command. He didn't want Rory to suspect that he was tagging along to protect the girl; they trailed her quietly, a unified team by all outward appearances. Once the dog stopped, and growled in their general direction; otherwise, they followed without being detected.

When they got to the marina, Ian breathed a sigh of relief: she was going to hop on a boat, and sail away. There was no chasing her over the water, making themselves an open target on the open sea. His heart fell when she returned to the dock after choosing a vessel. She hunted around, obviously looking for something, until she disappeared from view. The dog went with her.

"Come on," Rory hissed.

He headed for the boat. Ian followed, climbing aboard and keeping an eye out for her return. They waited until she came back, then waited for her in the cabin. Her footsteps sounded on deck, and the floor lurched under their feet. Ian felt Rory bump into him, resisted the urge to distastefully shove him away.

"I think she got under way," Ian frowned. His heart began to pound. "I can't swim."

Rory shushed him. "Ye won't have to," he whispered.

"Do you know how to sail?" Ian asked quietly.

"Nah." Rory's elbow found his ribs in the dark. "I know how to drive, though. This thing's got a motor, too; and a steering wheel."

There was a loud bark from the other side of the door, followed by a low growl. Rory shushed him again, although Ian froze at the sound. They could hear the young woman calling from on deck; her voice grew closer as her footsteps approached. A low click sounded, her hand falling on the handle from the other side. Ian felt Rory puff up beside him, and heard his voice as daylight flooded the little cabin.

"Hey girlie," Rory grumbled. "Guess who?"

Ian felt him move, waited another moment for his eyes to adjust. By the time he stepped out behind Rory, both man and dog were sprawled on the deck. Rory had his arm up, trying to fight off the giant beast, and the dog had that arm in its jaws. It was growling, and Rory was screaming; as Ian watched Rory brought up his other arm. The dog bit that too. Rory balled up his free fist and cocked it back against the deck.

Stepping forward, Ian kicked Rory's head like a soccer ball. Rory's head lolled, his fist dropped, and his eyes rolled back in his head. As he shook off the effects of the blow, Rory shot Ian a hateful glare.

Ian kicked him again. This time Rory went out; as soon as he did, the dog went for his throat. Blood puddled on the deck around Rory's head as it twitched with the dog's movements. It would have been a satisfying sight for Ian, had he seen it; it would have been even more satisfying for the young woman he had boarded the boat to save. Unfortunately, neither of them saw it. She was fumbling at the railing, trying to find purchase on the slippery surface after having backed up in surprise; and Ian was busy tumbling over the side of the boat, having lost his footing with that last satisfying kick to Rory's skull.

He splashed into the water, and gasped at the wet and the cold. Ian began to splash about and cry out, as he watched the boat continue to sail away. He made his case between desperate gulps of air and awkward sips of salted water.

"Please!" he shouted. "Please! I don't swim!"

The woman stepped to the rear of the vessel.

"You should have thought of that before getting on a boat!" she called back.

"Please!" Ian's eyes went wide as his head disappeared under the waves again. He gasped for air as he fought his way back to the surface. "Don't let me drown! Please!"

She turned and grasped the life preserver, tossed it toward him. Ian fought his way awkwardly through the water, grasping for it long before it came within reach. When his hand finally landed on the hard circle of foam, he watched her toss the line that had kept it tied to the boat into the water.

"No!" Ian cried out. "Come back! Please! I was only trying to help you! I swear it!"

He could barely make her out anymore; Ian doubted she could even hear him. She had rolled Rory's body over the side after throwing him the life preserver; after that, she seemed to have faced forward into her future and turned her back on his plight. In all honesty, Ian didn't blame her; he wasn't exactly rescuer material.

Looking over his shoulder, Ian could maybe see the shore; it might have just been a distant haze. It didn't really matter at this point; his mind was made up. Ian paddled toward Rory's body, watching it bob in the water as he struggled with the waves. He thought it was moving for a moment, but that was impossible: Rory had been face down in the water for several minutes now; the only real concern he needed to have was getting there before the blood drew the sharks. He would empty Rory's pockets, take all the pills he could shovel into his belly, and float away once and for all into a nice peaceful eternal slumber.

Ian just had to get to the body.

Paddling and kicking, hardly moving, Ian was pouring sweat by the time he laid a hand on Rory's shoulder. His chest was heaving with exhaustion, and his buzz was long since worn off. It took everything he had to pull the corpse toward him and turn it over in the water.

Rory came alive at his tug, lifting his head from the water and hissing at him in a ragged reptilian voice. Rory's eyes were the color of rusted red, and his biting teeth had grown long and jagged; he lurched forward in the water, splashing cold salty wetness and the stale stench of rotting flesh in Ian's face.

Ian sputtered, threw his arm up and felt Rory's teeth sink into his flesh. He opened his mouth to scream, only to swallow a gasp of water. His head sank under the waves one last time, as Rory's teeth found his shoulder; and the little bit of color that remained in Ian's world faded slowly to a full and final darkness.

ABOUT MICHELLE'S LUCK

How was that? Do you see why I avoided writing the end of that story? Although 'Ian's Shame' was started ninth, it was finished tenth. I liked Ian, and didn't want to see him die. It turned out that the story I jumped ahead to was hard in its own way, and made me realize that stories that take place in the midst of any apocalypse are going to feature some seriously unhappy endings.

So I went back and killed Ian.

It was still hard.

There is only one story that can claim to have been the first, and this next one is it. When I was writing Chapter Fifteen of 'Zombie Zero: The First Zombie', a question came up. This story answered that question, as did Ian's in its own way.

I'll tell you what that question was, in another form, after you read this story. Right now I want to talk about Michelle, and where she grew up. It was a lot different than where I grew up, and one's influence on the other is not at all the same as the other's influence on the one.

My first exposure to British comedy came late, when I was nearly an adult. After seeing all the Monty Python movies, I started seeking out more things to watch from across the pond. Some folks might have thought that my television set was broken for awhile there, since it seemed to only tune in to the BBC. I was glad for that period of obsession when it came time to write these stories. It helped me phrase the dialogue, and include some of the world otherwise being somewhat left out in the story.

I liked Ian, despite his bad choices. But I was very attached to Michelle, and looked forward to finishing her story when she came up in the queue. Michelle is in 'Zombie Zero: The First Zombie', in the italicized section at the beginning of Chapter 23. That snapshot actually takes place after this story, though; so don't feel rushed to find it now. Just know that this was the first story I got started on in this collection, and the anticipation built as the time came to finish it. It was completed eighth, in the most proper order I could see writing these at the time. It's being published now as the second-to-last volume because it is a real bonus for folks who have read 'Zombie Zero: The First Zombie'.

Thanks so much if that is you.

MICHELLE'S LUCK

Michelle wedged herself into the darkness, breathing as quietly as she could. She cringed internally as she curled bodily into a defensive ball. With her knees against her face, and her back against the wall, Michelle took long deep quiet breaths. Holding her breath was not an option, not after running for so long. She stared into the inky blackness, and hoped her long steady breaths wouldn't disturb her cover.

A door creaked open. Michelle felt her heart pounding in her chest; she struggled not to gasp for air. It was getting warm, under the tarp, and she was still breathing heavy. She bit her lip, swallowed her fear.

"Oy!" A voice called out, a man's voice. One of them.

"Let's have us a look in here." The same voice.

Breathing, hoping, waiting, Michelle kept herself as still as possible. Sweat started to bead up on her upper lip, and she switched to biting that one. Otherwise she stayed completely still, but for the slight rise and fall of her even breaths. Michelle wished she could enjoy the warmth of her shelter; she had been cold for days. Waiting out the apocalypse in an old abandoned castle had seemed like a good idea at first; then the cold had set into her bones, her torch had run out its batteries, and she had spent long dark shivering hours regretting her decision. She had gone out for food and blankets, finally; Michelle regretted that decision even more.

"See anything?" Another voice. Another one of them.

The tarp lit up suddenly, and she fought the urge to gasp. Instead she stayed quiet, breathing and listening.

"Nothing in here." The thin covering went dark.

"Did you look under that tarp?"

"Nah. Think she's under there?" The light came back.

"It's probably worth checking."

Michelle steeled herself, wishing they would just go away with every bit of her silent scared might.

"Are you hiding in there, pretty lady?" It was the first voice; Michelle could tell from his muddled accent. The other man spoke proper English. The end of the world had brought an end to the classes at last;

unfortunately, Michelle had yet to see any benefits.

She moved around as much as she dared, tracing her hands slowly around her on the floor. It had looked like some kind of tool shed from the outside; maybe there was something sharp or heavy nearby.

A foot fell heavily on the floor. Michelle felt the wood tremble underneath her. Her hand brushed against something cold and round.

"That tarp just moved." The proper one seemed to realize that his comrade needed him to point out the obvious. "She's under there."

"Nah," he drawled. "Probably a rat. They're bloody everywhere."

"Nonetheless," the Englishman responded, "do be careful."

Three more heavy footfalls, and Michelle clenched the hard object in her hand. She was holding her breath now. The tarp was pulled away, and a bright light blinded her.

"Well, I'll be," the man said, eyeing her. "You were right, Ian. Hey, pretty lady."

The beam of light went to her hand, and he laughed.

"What are you gonna do?" he sneered, his face as twisted as his accent. "Beat me with six inches of plastic pipe? Go ahead, girlie, take your best shot. Then I'll show you-"

She leapt to her feet, kicked him in the knee, hit him in the face with the pipe, then kicked him in the groin. He staggered backward, a red gash on his face. Michelle hit him with the pipe again as she dashed past him. The one he had called Ian shouldered her as she passed, hard, and grabbed her wrist with a viselike grip. Michelle's feet went out from under her, and she dropped the pipe.

The third man came up behind them as she struggled with Ian.

"Oy!" he hollered. "You found her!"

The third man's accent was definitely Irish; it sounded like he had a few beers in him somehow, despite it being the end of the world. He began to laugh uproariously as the man she had attacked stepped towards them. His torchlight was trained on the bloodied gash on the other man's face the entire time.

"Oy, Davey!" he laughed. "She got ya good, didn't she?"

"Just a scratch," Davey responded blithely. He put his face right up to hers as Michelle rose to her feet. "I'll get you for that."

Michelle took another swing at him. He

threw up his arm just as Ian tugged her other wrist, and her fist glanced off his elbow painfully.

"Bring her out here in the open," the last man said, "before she kicks both your asses."

Ian pulled her wrist again, hard, and tossed her to the ground. Michelle landed on soft grass. She immediately started clawing at the ground underneath her as she sat up and backed away, trying to get a handful of sand or dirt or rocks.

The three of them lined up shoulder to shoulder, looking down at her. Both of their torches were on her, like unwelcome spotlights.

Davey was in the middle, and the first to lean forward.

"Hey girlie," he sneered. "You know what I-"

There was a muffled thump, followed by another as Davey crumpled to the ground. Michelle was suddenly looking at a dead man's eyes, made eerily translucent by the light shining in them. His torch had fallen to the grass when he had, and it lay between them pointing at his face.

"What the hell?" the Irish fellow was nearly screaming. "What the hell was that?"

Michelle could see what it had been. The

light was not just shining on Davey's dead countenance: it was showing her the object that had struck him as well. It was a belt with bullets stacked two deep three quarters of the way around the leather, and a holster attached. The handle of a pistol was sticking out of the holster, and a little dot of blood was on one angled corner.

Lurching forward, she grasped the belt before they saw it. Michelle unsnapped the little leather strap that was keeping the gun holstered. Holding it up, she pointed it at Ian.

"Alright, now, hold on," he said, spreading his hands before him. He eyed Davey's lifeless body, made a move toward him. "Just because the cops are striking doesn't mean we can't be civilized toward each other. Just let me-"

"Back off," she said. Michelle held him in her sights.

Ian took a step back, while the other man began to snigger.

"Careful," he said, stepping forward. "You might accidentally-"

Michelle threw the safety and switched targets. Deliberately pointing near his feet, she fired off a round. He leapt backward.

"If I shoot you, it will not be an accident," she assured him.

A hungry howl split the air, from high above them. Michelle looked to the sky as the hairs on the back of her neck stood up. When she looked back, the men were gone.

Michelle sighed, grateful. She wasn't sure she would have been able to kill them, even if they were creeps. Kneeling, keeping her eyes on the shadows, she bent to pick up the belt. She wound it around her waist with one hand, keeping the pistol pointing forward. Once she had it fastened, she bent to pick up the fallen torch. She clicked it off, both to save batteries and to attract as little attention as possible. The lingering howl cut off just as her light did, and she looked to the sky once more.

There was nothing there but stars, and the faint crescent of a waning moon. Michelle moved toward the closest string of streetlights that she could see; she hoped there was food there, or water, or even just the peaceful warmth of a good night's sleep. She'd had enough of both humans and howlers for the night. Snugging the pistol in its holster, she walked slowly so it wouldn't slap loudly against her leg with each step.

* * *

Michelle crept to the window, and peered carefully inside. She couldn't believe there were lights on in the house; it had to be zombies. Peeking through the slightly parted curtains, she smiled at the sight beyond. By all appearances the family looked untouched by the end of the world. They sat on a sectional, the four of them, what appeared to be two parents and their two children. They had two bowls of popcorn, one between the children and the other on the man's lap. Every few moments, one of them would reach out and collect a few kernels. With the casual ease of people that had not missed a meal in their lives, they nibbled on the popped corn and watched the lighted screen together.

From where she was, Michelle was unable to see what they were watching. All she could see was their faces, relaxed and unafraid, and the bowls of puffed white. She had never been a huge fan of popcorn; yet her mouth filled with saliva as she stared at it. It looked so delicious, and they looked so normal; she almost kept moving.

Instead she stepped carefully along the outside wall, toward the front door. She would knock, she would ask for help, and she would hope against hope. After what she had been through, in her bedraggled state, Michelle wouldn't blame them if they turned her away. She crept along in the shadows until a strange flapping sound made her freeze in her tracks. Cocking her head, she listened.

It sounded like a ship's sail being buffeted loudly by the wind, flapping and cracking and getting closer. Michelle remained frozen in place, listening and watching the lighted lane. She almost gasped when she saw the source of the sound; she had to bite her lip to keep the exclamation inside. Floating smoothly along the power lines, a parachute whizzed through the flash of streetlights. Hanging from the network of thin cords was humanity's nightmare, a hungry howler dressed in bloodstained rags. It turned in flight as it descended, to disappear into the darkness of the yard behind the house.

It was the closest she had ever been to one of them, although it was only a glimpse. Michelle felt her hands tremble with more than the cold as the image burned itself into her brain. Quiet footfalls sounded in the back yard, and the flapping sounds culminated in a brief series of quieter flaps that ended in silence. The monster was on the ground.

There was no time to wonder what it

would do, or what she should do. In the next moment she heard the creature burst into the house, loudly turning the back door she couldn't see to so many splinters. Reversing her course, Michelle returned to the window. She peeked through just as she heard the first scream.

Loping into the living room, the creature never broke stride. It leapt to the part of the sofa that the children were sitting on, grabbed one child with razored talons and the other with rows of sharp biting teeth. It was a male, and looked a little too human to be written off completely as a monster. Michelle saw purpose in his movements, and intelligence in his rusted red eyes. He was startlingly fast, and he tore the children to shreds before either parent could lift themselves from their own cushions. Half of the sectional was stained stuffing, bloody spilt popcorn, and death.

Michelle looked down at the gun hanging at her hip. It looked so small. Nonetheless, she pulled it from the holster and gripped the handle with both hands. She chanced one last glance through the window before moving to the back door. The monster was eating the children, though they were long dead. He gnawed at one's arm while flaying the other's tender torso with his claws, lifting his head from one child to drop dripping strips of the other into his maw. He never stopped chewing, or moving, and he didn't seem to notice the couple behind him at all.

He was hitting the monster with a baseball bat; she was swinging a lamp awkwardly at the beast's back again and again. The zombie neither turned nor braced himself against the blows; he simply kept eating.

As quickly and quietly as possible, Michelle moved to the rear of the house. She tried to keep the image of the children she had seen go from peaceful to pieces from her mind. Holding the gun before her with both hands, she walked through the remains of the back door. She stepped carefully through the pieces on the floor, made her way up the short hallway. The end of the barrel was dancing in and out of the rear sight, and she realized that she was trembling uncontrollably. Michelle knew enough about pistols to throw a safety, and deliberately miss; she also knew that shaky hands did not make for accurate shooting.

Breathing deeply, quietly, she watched the tremble relax into a slow slight shakiness. She stepped into the living room, her gaze locked along the barrel. As she came to the end of the hallway, she froze. Backing away, she lowered the gun. For some reason she couldn't lower her eyes as she had the sights. Standing in the recessed darkness of the hallway, Michelle watched the horrific scene in terrified silence. The adults had turned to ramblers, and they were no longer fighting the howler. Michelle thought of all the news stories she had heard about both versions of the zombie outbreak, and how simply watching them interact spoke volumes.

The entire couch was splashed in blood, and small bits of every member of the family clung to the fabric. The howler was on top of them both on the couch, biting one and then the other with chilling ferocity. He ripped away a mouthful of flesh every time he dipped his head, and his face and front were painted a fresh shiny shade of red. Each of the ramblers opened their arms to his every bite, and smiled as he filled his mouth with their skin and sinew. A few feet away, the stripped skeletal remains of the children sat in the same pose they had been in before. They looked like they were still watching television. Bloody popcorn was everywhere, stuck to the bones and the blood and the howler's bloody arched back.

Michelle forced her feet backward, her

eyes still locked on the gruesome sight. The howler was visibly growing as it fed, and it paused to throw its head back and howl with hunger. Grasping the woman by the hair, he plunged her face into the man's belly. The last thing Michelle saw were the ridges beginning to rise on the woman's skull, and the way her limbs started to stretch. She was becoming a howler.

Once the image was blocked by a wall, Michelle turned and made for the back door. Outside, she used the light from the streetlamp to approach the single small structure in the backyard. Lowering herself carefully to her hands and knees, Michelle crawled to within a foot of the darkened doorway.

"Anybody in there?" she whispered. Michelle peered into the dark.

A low whimper issued from the doghouse, and a giant wet nose poked through the opening. Michelle felt her eyes go wide, but she didn't back away. Instead she leaned closer to the ground, spoke softly.

"Your family is getting eaten, sweetie," she cooed. "My family got eaten too. I think we should maybe be friends. What do you think? Hmmm?"

The dog's entire head came out of the

hole; Michelle had to resist the urge to draw back, or cry out: its head was enormous, bigger than hers. She smiled as best she could, and reached out her hand. Patting the giant furry skull, she murmured soft meaningless sounds. The dog moved forward some more, and licked her face.

A hungry howl came from inside the house, then another. Michelle threw a desperate glance over her shoulder, turned back to the dog. It had retreated back into the structure, and she could hear it whimpering.

"Listen, pup," she whispered. "I know we just met and all, but I was wondering if I might climb in there with you. I know you're big, but I won't take up much room. I sure could use a little heat."

That huge furry head came out again, and she could swear the dog was smiling. After panting in her face, then licking it once more, it retreated into the little structure.

Counting on her luck and the animal's good nature, Michelle crawled into the space. Immediately, the friendly creature pressed its huge body against hers, and she happily breathed in dog fur and odor as she soaked up its warmth. Huddling together, they waited in tense silence.

* * *

The dog growled, and Michelle pressed closer to him. She petted his shoulders where they were bunched together.

"What is it, buddy?" she whispered. "What do you see?"

Michelle moved her head so it was right next to the friendly creature's massive skull. Peeking out, her hand went still on his fur.

There were two of them now. The one from before looked bigger, his teeth and talons even more ridiculously long and threatening. The monster that had been a woman a few minutes ago stood at his side. They were looking at the doghouse together. One of them growled, and the dog growled back. The monster laughed, then howled. They turned together and ran off into the night.

Heaving a sigh, Michelle wrapped her arms around her furry companion. A thick warm wet tongue softly swiped her face, and she giggled.

"Come on," she said, wriggling out of the wide opening. She stood up, dusted her knees off, and beckoned. It was all she could do to not gasp as the creature followed her; it was huge. Michelle dropped to her knees, scratched about the dog's collar. Holding the tag, she read out loud under the light from the street.

"Mammoth," she said. Michelle looked over his huge furry body, the thick lines of muscles that stood out even in repose. "That's fitting. Hi, Mammoth."

He lunged at her, licking her face until Michelle was giggling and gasping for air. She stood up, went to the smashed doorway. In the kitchen, she stopped to look back; the dog had hesitated at the entrance, as if blocked by an invisible barrier. No matter how she beckoned or called softly to him, he would not cross the threshold. Even when she walked back to him, and tugged gently at his collar, he wouldn't move. He planted his bottom firmly on the door mat and harrumphed. Michelle pulled harder, and only succeeded in sliding herself across the smooth tiled floor. Exasperated, panting, she gave up and returned to the kitchen.

The first shelf she opened had chocolate bars in it. Michelle grabbed one, tore it open, and bit off a huge chunk. She heard a whimper from the doorway. Shaking her head, she called out through the mouthful.

"Sorry, big guy," she said. "No chocolate for you."

She took another bite, before she had quite swallowed the first, and opened the refrigerator with her free hand.

"How about cheese?" Michelle called out. "Doggies can have cheese."

Her voice was still muffled by the chocolate, but he seemed to know that word. Mammoth whimpered at the doorway while she grabbed a bottle of sparkling water and drank straight from the glass container. Reaching in with her other hand, Michelle grabbed a hunk of wrapped cheddar. She set the water on the counter, uncapped, and began to remove the plastic covering. More whimpering accompanied the smell of cheese as it filled the air. Michelle moved toward the doorway.

"Hey buddy," she said, dropping to her knees just beyond his reach. "You want some cheese?"

Mammoth looked at her. He panted, he smiled, he pressed against the invisible barrier. He wanted some cheese. Michelle felt bad, holding it just out of his reach; after a minute she tore off a hunk, fed it to him and bit a chunk off herself. She stood.

"Mammoth," she said through the cheese. "I know you take the rules very seriously. You're an outside dog; I get it.

But your family is gone, buddy. It's time to change the rules, okay?"

He was either being very attentive because he understood the importance of her tone, or he really wanted more cheese. Michelle broke off another piece, fed it to him. She stepped back further from him.

"Mammoth," Michelle said, "new rule: you are not to let me out of your sight. Do you understand?"

He barked, and whimpered again. One of his paws reached out, scraped at the threshold.

"The new rule supersedes all old rules," Michelle added, hopefully.

In one fluid motion, Mammoth lifted his considerable bulk to his full height; he walked to her side, looked up at her and started panting. Michelle knelt to pet him, and feed him another little chunk of cheese. She popped the last piece in her mouth, chewed it while grinning at him and scratching his ears vigorously.

"Good boy!" she grinned. He licked her face. Suddenly he went down on his front knees, raised his hackles and barked. Michelle stood just as suddenly, startled; she turned to see what he was looking at.

Moaning, twitching, the man that had

just lost his family and his humanity was staggering toward them. One of his arms was nothing but dangling bones, held together by loose scraps of sinew. His shoulders were both gone, and the fleshy arm hung and twitched as uselessly as the stripped bones. His feet didn't leave the floor when he walked, but dragged slowly across the tiles. Mammoth barked again.

"Careful, boy," Michelle said, backing toward the smashed back door. As soon as she moved past him, the dog launched himself at the rambler. Michelle was afraid he recognized his previous owner, and was moving in to be petted. He was enormous, and she had only known him a little while, but she didn't see the big friendly fellow as having a violent bone in his body. As they tumbled to the floor together, Michelle realized that she was wrong. Mammoth bit and clawed at the rambler, his movements a rapid blur of violence. It was all the monster could so to lay on his back and hold his arms defensively in front of him while chunks of his rotting flesh were tossed about like wet confetti.

Michelle stepped carefully around them, knelt by the rambler's head and pulled the pistol from its holster. The barrel trembled as she pointed it; she had to tell herself that it wasn't really a person, and close her eyes at the last second, to pull the trigger. As her ability to hear was suddenly overwhelmed by a loud ringing in her head, Michelle opened her eyes and pulled the trigger again. Finally, half of its brains exposed in a bloody mess and the other half spread across the carpet, the monster lay still. Mammoth began panting, and smiling; he took two quick steps and licked the tears from Michelle's face.

"Good boy, Mammoth," she sputtered, wrapping her arms about his wide ribcage. She buried her face in his fur, let the tears come. He panted heavily and happily in her embrace.

* * *

Michelle found a room in the back with a bed big enough for the both of them and a widescreen television on the dresser. She threw blankets over the stained remains that were strewn about the living room, and locked herself in the bedroom with Mammoth. They snacked on cheese and popcorn, watching the news at low volume until they fell asleep. After a few hours she woke up, gasping for air; for a few minutes she couldn't tell if she was dreaming or if she had awaken in a lethal termite fumigation. Then she saw Mammoth looking at her sheepishly, and realized what effect the cheese had had on his digestion; she had buried her face under the blankets, and gone back to sleep.

More hours passed, then the rest of the day. It was late into the following night when she woke refreshed and renewed. Michelle snuck into the kitchen, found him some proper food that wouldn't turn the bedroom into a gas chamber again, and let him out to do his business in the yard. She showered and dressed in some dark clothes that she found in the closet, and watched the news quietly with him until the first rays of light replaced the chilling hungry howls that sounded throughout the night.

Picking up the remote, Michelle paused as a different feed cut in suddenly.

"Attention survivors," A man's voice said. The screen was blank. "We have found a cure."

Michelle listened intently to the entire broadcast, then shut off the television and went to the closet once more. She packed a backpack halfway full with a change of clothes, then went to the kitchen to heft the rest of the bag of dog food. It took some shoving, and a little good old fashioned cursing, but finally she stuffed the bag in the bag and slung it over one shoulder. She burdened one pocket of her sweatshirt with granola bars and the other with chocolate, grabbed a fresh bottle of sparkling water, and headed out.

It was a different thing to walk the streets with an enormous dog at her side and a giant pistol hanging from her belt. What folks she saw gave them a wide berth, and the ramblers were easily outrun by their brisk walking pace. The news broadcasts had said that the howlers only hunted at night; Michelle was counting on it. She talked to Mammoth while she walked, to comfort him or herself.

"I've lived here in England my whole life," she told him. Mammoth glanced at her, panted and nodded for her to go on.

"Except summers," she smiled, her eyes on the road ahead while her mind drifted to the past. "Summers I spent with my dad, in the States. Actually, we went all over the world; but he lived in California. He was so different from my mum. She was uptight and proper, and he was just a fun and happy guy."

Michelle laughed, glanced over at him.

He was panting lightly, keeping pace with her effortlessly.

"Listen to me," she frowned. "I keep talking about them both like they're dead. I don't know that. Maybe they're both safe. Maybe they're both fine."

"Yeah," she muttered. "And maybe they decided to try having a relationship after all this time. Maybe they got married and moved to Hawaii, and they're just waiting for us to show up and live with them."

Glancing at him again, Michelle laughed quietly.

"That's what I used to want, you know," she confided. "When I was a little girl I just wanted my parents to get together and get married. I almost never saw them together, but they were always nice to each other. They never said an unkind word about each other. I didn't get it, until I was older. They didn't get together to start a family all those years ago. They got together to get together, for the fun of being together. When I asked my mum what she saw in him, she always said that he was fun and different. When I asked Dad, he would always say 'Your mom was a beautiful and fascinating woman; she still is.'"

Michelle patted his head as they walked;

he was so tall, she didn't have to stoop or bend over.

"I realized how strange it would have been for both of them to be together a long time ago," she sighed. "Their lives were so different, they would have both had to give up so much. I wouldn't actually be happy if they were together and unhappy. You know?"

She looked over, and he nodded again. She scratched his head.

"Maybe I should have just gotten a dog," she giggled. "This is better than friends, or therapy, or a boyfriend. Believe me, I know; I've tried them all."

Adjusting the straps of the knapsack so they would dig into a different part of her shoulder, shifting as she walked, Michelle went on.

"That wouldn't have worked, though," she mused. "I wouldn't have gotten you; and even if I'd had you, I would have had to be away from you when I left the country. Humans can carry all kinds of nasty stuff across borders, but pets are not an easy thing to travel with. I suppose that's the bright side to all this 'end of the world' nonsense; I can take you on a boat with me."

Mammoth stopped suddenly, planting

his feet on the sidewalk. He sniffed the air, panted, looked up at her and panted a little more.

Michelle sighed, looked around. She went back to him, knelt at his side. Setting the backpack on the sidewalk, she unzipped the main compartment and took out his bowl. She had another cautious look around before uncapping a bottle of water and pouring some in.

"There you go, big guy," she smiled, scratching him lightly about the ears. Before capping the bottle, she sipped at it herself. "Drink up."

He raised one eyebrow, panted dog breath in her face.

"Come on, buddy," Michelle urged him. "We need to get going."

Mammoth looked at her, panted.

"Mammoth," she pleaded. "Drink some water."

He bent, dutifully, and licked at the bowl. He raised his head, licked her face. Michelle giggled.

"Drink up," she said again, nodding at the bowl.

He dipped his head, took one more halfhearted swipe with his tongue.

Michelle overturned the bowl, let the

last remaining droplets spill into the street. She dried it on her shirt, stuffed it back in the knapsack and stood up. After taking a few steps, she turned and called to him.

"Mammoth!" she frowned. "Let's go."

He stood there, panting. Michelle went back to him.

"What's the matter?" she asked. "Are you afraid of boats?"

His eyebrow shot up again. She laughed.

"My dad taught me to sail, and navigate," she said. "It will be safer on the water than on land. There's a cure for this terrible thing that's happening. If there's a cure, that means there's a community dedicated to surviving all this. I want to find them. I want to help them, if I can."

He wouldn't budge. Michelle threw up her hands.

"Fine," she sputtered, exasperated. "I'm going."

She hadn't taken three more steps before he caught up to her. He kept stride with her. Neither of them looked over at each other. After a few minutes, she pointed and spoke.

"There's the marina," she said. "You can pick our boat, if you want."

Mammoth ran ahead when they got close, choosing a floating path and dashing to the end.

"A sailboat, buddy," Michelle called out. "We need a sailboat."

He backtracked, stopped before another vessel. Michelle caught up, stood beside him on the drifting dock. She sized up his choice.

"Alright," she nodded. "Small, but not too small. It looks new enough; it probably has state of the art navigation, and a trolling motor in case we run out of wind. It looks like we can both stand up in the cabin, too. Let's check it out."

Michelle hopped over the water, grasped a rung on the ladder, and looked back at him.

"Oh," she said. "Hang on a minute, big guy."

She climbed on deck, slung the pack from her back and lowered it to the smooth sanded surface. Michelle tried the handle on the door; it was unlocked. She stepped into the enclosed space, nodded, and stepped out.

Climbing down the ladder again, she leapt to land beside Mammoth.

"Good pick," she said, kneeling beside him to scratch behind his ears. "Now let's go find us a way to get you up on deck, okay? I can't lift you; I'd be willing to bet that you weigh more than I do."

Michelle spent awhile looking through the other vessels in the marina and poking around the nearby buildings. Mammoth trotted along beside her, smiling happily enough. She found a board pretty early, long and wide enough for him to walk on; but when she stretched it between boat and dock, and stepped on it, it bowed precariously as she placed her second foot. Michelle pulled the board back to the dock, so he wouldn't be tempted to step onto it, and went searching for something better.

Finally she had it: she found a ladder that she could lay across the gap, and lay the board over that. The board fit across the width of the rungs, and was held in place by the slight rise of the uprights where they attached to each step. She dropped the ladder into place the first time with a loud bang that echoed across the water; when she put the wood in place, it slid toward her. Michelle had to yank the ladder back onto the deck, splashing the top step in the water, and turn it around; then the board was held in place by gravity and the top step, which was marked to let her know that it was not a step.

He dashed right up it when she got the whole thing figured finally. Rather than go out on deck, or play king of the world, he rushed to the closed cabin door. Sniffing at it, he barked. He looked at her, and barked again.

"I know, buddy," Michelle nodded. "I'm tired too. Let's get away from shore far enough so we can't see it before we dry to drop anchor or drift for the night. Okay?"

He whimpered, and sniffed at the door again. When she moved, he stayed with her, as she kicked down the rudder and set the tiller. She hoisted the sails, tugging the halyards into place and tying them to the cleat hitch. Casting off just in time, she smiled as Mammoth swayed and finally found his footing. Michelle went to the foredeck and let the salty breeze kiss her face. She turned back, called out to him.

"Hey, big guy," she said. "Come up here, see where we're headed."

Honestly, there wasn't much to see but blue sky and green water stretching off into forever; that didn't mean it wasn't one of her favorite sights. Whether she associated the open sea with her father or freedom didn't matter to Michelle. It only mattered that the view always brought a smile to her face and a lift to her heart. She took a step back towards him, called out again.

"Mammoth," she cooed. "Come here, buddy."

He growled, then whimpered. Finally, he turned a slow lumbering circle and settled his considerable bulk in front of the cabin door.

Michelle sighed, looked behind them and then before them; she headed back to kneel at his side.

"Okay," she said, scratching at his ears. "Let's go take a nap. I know it's been a long day, and you're probably used to a good half a dozen naps by this point on most days. I suppose I could use one too."

When her hand fell on the door handle, he barked and backed up. Michelle bent, petted him, and turned the handle.

"Hey girlie." A voice came from the darkness. "Guess who?"

*   *   *

Michelle backed up, nearly losing her footing. As two shady shapes became the forms of two men advancing on her, everything became a blur to her. She backed up further, half-stumbling, until she hit the railing. She heard barking, and growling, punctuated by screaming. By the time Michelle had reoriented herself, one man had either jumped or been chased overboard; the other was on the wooden deck. Mammoth had his throat in his jaws; he was still growling, and shaking his head violently back and forth, but the man was clearly done fighting for his life. A thick puddle of blood was widening under his head and shoulders, and his eyes stared lifelessly into the distance.

She heard the other man calling out from the water.

"Please!" he shouted. "Please! I don't swim!"

Michelle exchanged a look with Mammoth.

"You should have thought of that before getting on a boat!" she called back.

"Please!" His eyes went wide as his head disappeared under the waves. He gasped for air as he came back into view. "Don't let me drown! Please!"

She glanced at Mammoth again. He was panting, smiling, his mouth ringed in blood. He barked, happily enough.

"Oh, hell," Michelle muttered.

She walked to the railing, grasped the life preserver and tossed it as far toward him as she could. Unwrapping the safety line, she watched it drift away behind them as the wind pushed their little boat closer to the sunset. She rolled the bloody corpse to the back of the boat, and shoved him off the side; smiling, she turned to Mammoth.

"I thought I was saving you," she breathed. "But you keep on saving me. Thanks, big guy. You ready for a nap?"

Mammoth barked, and moved toward her as she knelt to love on him.

"Oh, no," Michelle giggled, turning her head as he tried to lick her face. "Let's get you all cleaned up, and get a little food in your belly. Then you can lick your new mama's face all you want, buddy. Okay?"

He nodded, once, and stood patient for her while she sponged the blood from his fur. They both ate everything in their bowls, and by the time they were done the sun had nearly set. Michelle shut everything down for the night, and dropped anchor; she was pleased when the ship stopped drifting. It would not always be that way.

Cuddling up with Mammoth, she found she could not nod off right away. Instead she talked to him, telling him what it was like in other countries and lightly stroking his fur. Long after he had begun snoring loudly, deeply ensconced in a peaceful still sleep,

Michelle talked to him about where they would go and what they would do when they reached America. She was glad the end of the world had brought them together.

ABOUT MONSTER BREAKUP

Were you rooting for Michelle, even knowing how things would pretty much turn out? I sure was. Ian's story came first so you might get where he was coming from, but it's still hard to feel bad for the guy from her perspective. Watching Michelle's luck save her again and again was one of the few bright spots for me in the 'Year of the Zombie'.

Besides using real life people to flesh out the character sheet in 'The First Zombie' and 'The Last Zombie', I also featured a couple of real life canines. Mammoth is the giant dog that my partner Dawn raised from a puppy; in our world, he's our dog. In the world of 'Zombie Zero', he was born in Europe. His family was not a European version of us; I thought it would be weird to put the author or publisher of the books into the books. Mammoth, though...well, I needed I giant dog that could throw down if he needed to.

The other canine that is featured in 'Zombie Zero: The Last Zombie' is not as physically robust as Mammoth, but he's formidable in his own way.

Lefty is a good friend's dog, who gets along great with Mammoth in our world. He's also part wolf, which takes the whole 'throwing down' thing to a whole new level. I'm glad I've never had to see either of them get after anyone in real life, but it was fun to watch them play that role in 'Zombie Zero'.

Remember that question I was talking about earlier, the one that made me start writing Michelle's story in the first place? Well, I was writing 'Zombie Zero: The First Zombie'; and a certain someone kicked a pistol out of an airplane. It made me wonder: what happened to that pistol? You might have the opposite question rolling around in your head at this point, something like this: where the hell did that pistol come from?

Well, I'm not spoiling it. If you have read 'Zombie Zero: The First Zombie', then you just got a rewarding tie-in, and maybe an answer to a question that I had as well. If not...well, you might consider it. It will give you a little more context for this next story too, whichever you read first. This is a huge tie-in, although it is quite short, that didn't belong in the bigger books. Allen is a main character, and this is one of those terrible/wonderful things that happened to him between the chapters of 'The First Zombie'.

MONSTER BREAKUP

Allen had counted four heat signatures in the house. They were human; he could smell their fresh flesh on the drifting wind. He pulled the parachute handles into a smooth flare, and stepped from the sky to the earth with three unhurried footfalls. Unclipping the harness holding him about the legs and chest, he let the flapping fabric drift away in the wind. Hunger twisted at his belly, and he let his recent thoughts be devoured by the painful ache. The back door splintered under his powerful talons, and he streaked through the tiled kitchen to burst howling into the living room.

The two little heat signatures on the sofa nearest him opened their mouths to scream; before they could, he was upon them. They were but a few tender bites each, hard won bites punctuated by blows from behind. He gnawed at them long after they had given up their lives, and most of their flesh. Allen turned when he was finished, swept the woman and the lamp she was swinging aside, and pounced on the man. His baseball bat fell quietly to the carpet, striking the floor at the same time as his skull. Allen opened his mouth unnaturally wide and sheared off a third of the man's shoulder. His mouth was flooded with sinew and blood, and his skull reverberated with the sounds of his teeth grinding bone to powder.

Allen kept eating, even when the woman picked up the baseball bat and began pounding his wide muscled back with it. He had nearly consumed the man's entire arm; the man kept reaching out to him with it, after he started to turn, shoving his own flesh into Allen's mouth. Finally the pounding of the bat began to annoy him; Allen tossed them both on the couch, bit her and then him again. Once the change took her, they were both reaching out to him with bloody offerings torn from their own bodies. He felt his power growing like his monstrous body.

Grasping a handful of the man's flesh, he stuffed it into the woman's mouth. She chewed, then smiled as a new row of sharp jagged teeth pushed out the old. He pressed her face into the man's belly, and felt her skull take new armored shape as his talons held her head to the feast. When he pulled her away, she turned to him and grinned. She was still chewing, and smiling, as Allen stood and wiped his own dripping mouth on his sleeve. When he moved away from the bloody mess that used to be her family, she followed. Without so much as a glance backward, she trailed him through the kitchen and out to the back yard.

He could hear her thoughts, what little there was to hear; he could sense her hunger. Allen scanned the area, sniffed at the air. There was heat in the doghouse, and the distinct smell of human. The little space was one big burning red heat signature to his eyes, and he stepped closer; a growl started in the hot shadowy structure. He laughed.

Allen felt a tug on his hand. He looked down: her monstrous digits were intertwined with his. He brought his rusted red eyes up, to meet hers; they flashed with hunger, and she howled. It was too much to resist, her screaming twisting hunger and strange monstrous beauty. He howled as well, and let go of her hand. Dropping to all fours, he showed her how they could move, and run. She chased him past the next house, and the next; then they doubled back and ate her neighbors. They heard a gunshot as they feasted, followed almost immediately by another; they hardly paused at the sounds.

His companion completed her

transformation while she ate, and they had both had their fill before they were finished. One little boy remained, mindlessly rambling about the living room and bumping randomly into things. Allen tossed the kid over his shoulder and raced her to the next house. She held the lone occupant down while the child fed; suddenly Allen realized that they had formed a little zombie family. They hunted together, eating and turning humans as the tide of their hunger ebbed and flowed; and their little family grew. Most of the adults that they turned went off on their own, but more and more children stayed with them as the night wore on. She would smile at him while she fed, and hold his hand while she watched the children eat; despite their lack of words, they were connected in the most primal way.

By the time dawn broke the starry sky into stabbing rays of early light, they had somewhere between forty and fifty children hunting with them. It was hard to count, in the confusing rush of bodies and constant bursts of blood. The group's hunger acted as one beastly appetite; they moved from residential streets to scour the countryside, never quite slaking their collective need. No was was left alive, or unchanged.

More than one child cried out as the sunlight speared at sensitive rusted eyes; Allen led them to a castle that smelled like the last human had left a couple days ago. They piled into an unlit inner chamber, twisting their bodies into one huge contorted mess of unnaturally long limbs, sharp jagged teeth and long razored talons. Allen found himself at the center of it all, wrapped in her arms and pressed about on all sides by little monsters. It felt eerily comforting to him, and Allen let himself drop into an exhausted slumber in the midst of the murderous dozing hive.

*   *   *

He woke before evening fell, coming conscious in the same mess of tumbled bodies. Allen's hunger was back, and so were the thoughts that had driven him unrelentingly forward. He looked over the pile of creatures as he extricated himself from them, torn between his disgust for them and his disdain for himself. Breaking free of them, Allen moved away and watched them sleep.

For days, he hadn't looked into a mirror. It was much easier to watch himself tear apart strangers from an inside view; seeing what he actually looked like from the outside would be too much. Yet this heap of snoring monsters was exactly what he had been trying to avoid by steering clear of reflective surfaces; they were a perfectly clear outpicturing of his horrific new life. His stomach turned as he watched them sleep, his hunger for once forgotten.

She stirred, reached out in her sleep to the spot he had just left empty. Her eyes came open, rusted red and hungry, and she rose slowly to move to his side. She watched the children with him, and he felt her experiencing the savage sight in a completely different way than he was.

Allen felt her hand reach out, her taloned fingers entwine with his. He glanced over at her, and she smiled. Half of her face was her mouth, and it was filled with teeth. There was more than one chunklet of flesh caught between her jagged biters, rotting as time passed.

Trying not to convey his disgust, Allen disengaged. He stepped away. She followed, grasped his hand again. Glancing at the pile of sleeping monsters, she spoke.

"Family," she said. It was horrific, barely a word.

Allen held up one finger, put it to his

lips. He nodded toward the children, to let them sleep. Pulling her by the hand, he stepped out of the room and into the next. There were candy wrappers and castoff clothing on the floor, the only evidence that anyone had been here in the last century. He stepped over them, stopped in the center of the room and faced her. Rather than speak, and solicit more disgusting sounds from her toothy maw, Allen projected his thoughts to her mind. It was a clear series of pictures: him, wandering streets and alleys and countryside, alone. There were no children behind him in the images, no monster love at his side.

At first the images startled her. Allen wanted to explain; she could communicate with any other member of their destructive family. If it had a taste for human flesh, its mind was in the same hive network as yours. He couldn't think of an image to project that might send the message; he tried a word.

"Bond," he growled. His voice was horrific, monstrous, appalling. Allen cringed at the sound of it. He would not attempt another word.

She nodded, fervently, took his other hand.

"Yes," she breathed. "Bond."

She stepped toward him, raised herself up to kiss him.

Allen pulled back, dropped her hands, turned away.

She dropped to all fours, ran a dizzying circle around him, and stopped in front of him.

She stood, reached out her hand.

Allen brushed it away.

She mewled, waved her hand in the direction of the children.

"Bond," she growled again. "Family."

Allen sighed. He opened his arms to her. She leapt forward, grasped him about the waist. Cupping her thick skull with his powerful clawed fingers, he pressed her face gently to his chest. He held her for a full minute, stroking the ridge that ran along the top of her hairless skull. When he pulled away, there were red stained tracks of blood where both of her cheeks used to be.

Cupping her face between his hands, Allen smiled at her. He leaned forward, touched his mouth to her tears. He kissed her forehead lightly, then her mouth. Then he twisted her skull, quickly.

Her head turned sideways; her body twitched, still holding him.

Allen twisted again. It was harder this

time; but he was strong: the motion was accompanied by a satisfying crack, and her arms went limp around his waist. He kept turning her head, until the skin broke and it came free in his hands. Blood spurted all over his face, and Allen turned away in disgust; one red droplet was a tear.

The body dropped to the floor at his feet, still twitching. Allen let her head fall from his hands, kicked it away from the corpse.

He crept to the door, peered into the room.

They were all sleeping, still piled together in a monstrous clump. One of them raised her head while he watched, blinking rusted red eyes sleepily before looking at him.

Allen smiled, put one finger to his lips as he had earlier, and sent her an image of her repulsive little body relaxed in deep sleep. She smiled, closed her eyes, and burrowed deeper into the carnivorous hive.

It was an image that was to haunt him for days, that pile of little living corpses. She had been right to see what they had done the way she had. What had they been doing together, if not building a family?

Drifting off into the night, alone, Allen let the monster within have what was left of his will. His razored talons swam in hot blood time and again; somehow it was her blood he thought of with each kill. It had surely been washed from his hands in the red river; yet somehow her blood still stained his mind, and each stranger's screaming hot splash brought his monstrous mind back to her.

He wondered more than once where the children were, how they had reacted to finding her corpse in the next room. Allen didn't reach out to the little terrors with his mind; but he did think of them nearly as much as he did her. Becoming a flesh-eating zombie had made Allen realize that he had never truly been honest with himself in his human life. Thinking of the children, and of her, he realized that he had gone from being an inadequate human to failing even as a monster.

Allen drowned his thoughts in hot splashes of blood, mouthfuls of pulsing flesh, and the resounding cracking of bones.

Dear reader,

I hope you loved 'Monster Break-up'! It was much like 'Zombie Zero: The First Zombie' in its pacing and its stark contextual feel. I might have ordinarily ended with a longer offering, but I wanted to leave you with the dramatic feel and ending of Allen's story. I don't just hope you loved this one, of course; I hope you loved all of them! Any way I can get you to spread the word a little?

If you leave a review on Amazon or Goodreads for this book, that is always very much appreciated. There is a tutorial on my website for anyone who would like a little guidance on writing a book review.

It's even easier to join the 'Secret Society of Deeper Meaning', and I appreciate that more than you might guess. You can even send me a message, at that email address under my name. It might take awhile for me to get back to you, since I keep myself pretty busy; but I will get back to you.

The special sharing that I sensed as a reader is more important to authors than I was ever able to imagine. There is a sacred bond that forms every time someone enjoys something I wrote, and that bond means more to me than I ever thought possible.

That's why I say 'thanks for reading' so much; I'm actually really glad that you did.

There is one more book in the short story volumes, set to release a month after this one. I hope you pick it up, and that you love reading it. In the meantime, did you know that this isn't my first series of books? There's another trilogy that I wrote, and you might like it even more than the zombie stories. I love some of the comparisons it gets, but I love it even more when someone says it's like nothing they've ever read before.

That kind of how I felt, writing it.

All the information on the trilogy should be somewhere in the next few pages, as well as my first book. You can find the first few chapters of any of my books for free on my website, and feel free to follow the circuitous rabbit hole that is my weekly blog. If you do all this, or even any of it, you know what's coming next. You also know that I say it because I mean it.

Thanks for reading!

All the best,

Jay

Jay@JayNorry.com

Twitter: @JayNorry

The Secret Society of Deeper Meaning

Also available from J.K. Norry. . .

<u>Zombie Zero</u>
Zombie Zero: The First Zombie
Zombie Zero: The Last Zombie

<u>Zombie Zero: The Short Stories</u>
Volume 1: The Sickness Spreads
Volume 2: The Beginning of the End
Volume 3: Love Lost at Sea
Volume 4: The Zombie Killers
Volume 5: Monstrous Consequences
Volume 6: The Heart of the Monster

<u>The Walking Between Worlds trilogy</u>
Demons & Angels (Book I)
Rise of the Walker King (Book II)
Fall of the Walker King (Book III)

<u>As Jay Norry</u>
Stumbling Backasswards Into the Light

Learn more about the author at
www.JayNorry.com